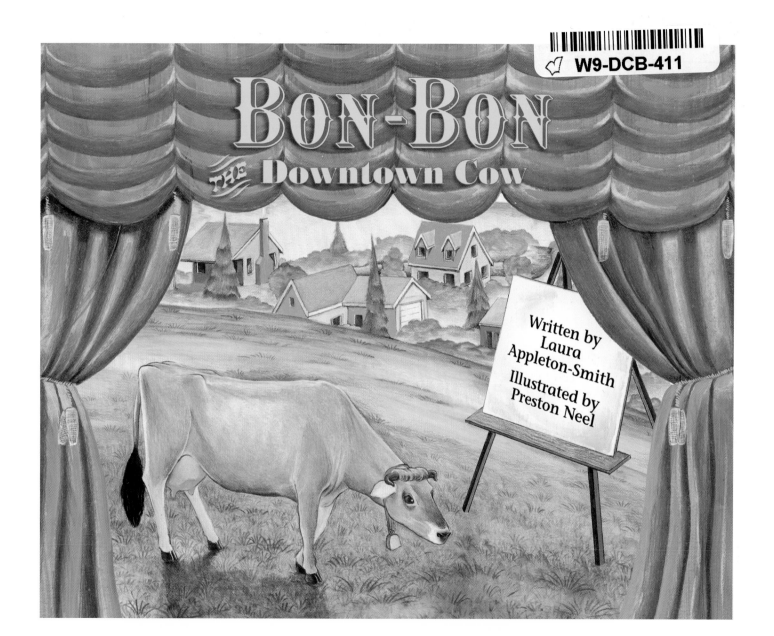

Bon-Bon

THE Downtown Cow

Written by
Laura
Appleton-Smith

Illustrated by
Preston Neel

Laura Appleton-Smith was born and raised in Vermont and holds a degree in English from Middlebury College. Laura is a primary schoolteacher who has combined her talents in creative writing and her experience in early childhood education to create *Books to Remember*. Laura lives in New Hampshire with her husband Terry.

Preston Neel was born in Macon, GA. Greatly inspired by Dr. Seuss, he decided to become an artist at the age of four. Preston's advanced art studies took place at the Academy of Art College San Francisco. Now Preston pursues his career in art with the hope of being an inspiration himself; particularly to children who want to explore their endless bounds.

A Book to Remember™

Published by Flyleaf Publishing
Post Office Box 287, Lyme, NH 03768

For orders or information, contact us at **(800) 449-7006**.
Please visit our website at **www.flyleafpublishing.com**

First Edition
Library of Congress Catalog Card Number: 2002090761
Hard cover ISBN: 1-929262-09-4
Soft cover ISBN: 1-929262-10-8

For Terry

LAS

━

For Eve Elizabeth Neel

PN

As the sun crept up past the hills around the town,
the day at The Brown Farm was beginning.

As the rest of the town slept,
Farmer Brown milked his cow Bon-Bon.

Outside, Mrs. Brown fed the ducks and pigs.

The mist drifted on the pond and the sun glinted on the wet grass.

But as Farmer Brown milked,
his cow Bon-Bon hung her lip down so far
it just about hit the ground.

It was as if Bon-Bon was pouting.

"Bon-Bon is so glum.
Perhaps she is ill,"
Farmer Brown told
Mrs. Brown as he led Bon-Bon
out to the barnyard.

The fact was that Bon-Bon
was not ill, but she did have
a problem...

The problem was that
Bon-Bon did not want
to be just a cow.
She wanted to be a singer.

Bon-Bon wanted to be a star.

Bon-Bon's problem began the night the barn owl
told her about his visit to the downtown bandstand.

He told her about the singer–about how her gown glinted
as she bowed under the bandstand lights.

"Wow... If I could sing one night on a bandstand in front of a crowd I would be so proud. But that will not happen. I am just a cow."

From that night on, when the Browns
and the rest of the farm animals were tucked in bed,
Bon-Bon snuck out of her pen.

Under the stars and the barnyard light,
Bon-Bon sang her songs into the night.

ACT 3

One sun-up (a sun-up that Bon-Bon would never forget),
there was a loud racket in the barnyard.

The ducks quacked at the pigs.
The pigs grunted at the dogs.
The dogs howled at the cats.

"What is the fuss?" Farmer Brown asked as he milked.

When Bon-Bon was let out, the ducks were flapping their wings at a brown bag that was pinned to the farm wagon.

It had, "TALENT CONTEST TONIGHT" printed on it.

"At ten o'clock under the stars and the barnyard light," yowled the cats.

"A talent contest! Who planned it?"
Bon-Bon asked as her pout lifted into a big grin.

Not an animal could tell her.

Bon-Bon did not have a second to stop.
She and the rest of the animals had to plan their acts.

The dogs met next to the farm plow.
They sang songs by howling and growling and bow-wowing.

The ducks went down to the pond.
They quacked and flapped their wings as they swam around and around.

The cats met in the barn loft.
They bounded around and did fantastic acrobatic tricks.

The hogs and sows clowned around in a mound of mud;
their snouts grunted loud pig sounds.

What a hubbub!

Farmer Brown contacted the vet.
He asked her to visit as fast
as she could.

"The animals must be sick,"
he fretted.

The vet inspected the crowd animal by animal.
They were all fit and well as far as she could tell.

"It must be too hot outside. Put the animals in the barn until tonight," the vet instructed Farmer Brown.

It was just as well...
The animals rested and planned their acts.

Bon-Bon found a flour sack to put on.
It was not a gown, but it would be
an outfit for her act.

ACT 4

At ten o'clock the animals met at the farm wagon under the barnyard light.

There was a crowd of skunks and rabbits and squirrels— as well as all of the farm animals.

There were more animals than Bon-Bon could count!

It was a fantastic talent contest.
The acts were fun and acrobatic;
but the best act was the last...

Bon-Bon the Downtown Cow was a hit.

The crowd quacked and yowled and grunted and howled for more.

Bon-Bon bowed.

The owl was proud.

Just then Farmer Brown's
light clicked on.

The animals scattered.
They ran back to their pens
and into the hills.

Farmer Brown inspected the barn.
The animals were all tucked in their pens.

"It has not been the best day," Farmer Brown grumbled
as he clicked off the barn light.

But for Bon-Bon, it had been the best day...
Bon-Bon had been the Downtown Cow.

From that day on, Bon-Bon was a different cow.
She was proud of herself.

She felt that the talent contest was a gift
that had been planned just for her;
but she never found out *who* planned it.

Did you?

Bon-Bon the Downtown Cow is decodable with the 26 phonetic alphabet sounds plus the "ou" and "ow" phonograms, and the ability to blend those sounds together. Words with the "ar" phonogram are also used and can be introduced either as a new phonogram or as Puzzle Words.

Puzzle Words are words used in the story that are either irregular or may have sound/spelling correspondences that the reader may not be familiar with.

The **Puzzle Word Review List** contains Puzzle Words that have been introduced in in previous books in the *Books to Remember* Series.

Please Note: If all of the words on this page are pre-taught and the reader knows the 26 phonetic alphabet sounds, plus the phonograms listed above, and has the ability to blend those sounds together, this book is 100% phonetically decodable.

Puzzle Words:	Puzzle Word Review List:		"ou" words:	"ow" words:
all	a	than	about	bow-wowing
been	as	that	around	bowed
day	be	the	bounded	Brown
forget	began	their	count	Browns
herself	by	then	flour	Brown's
more	could	there	found	clowned
Mrs.	for	they	ground	cow
told	from	to	loud	crowd
who	front	tonight	mound	down
	have	too	out	downtown
	he	want	outfit	gown
	her	wanted	outside	growling
	I	was	pouting	how
	into	were	pout	howled
	is	what	proud	howling
	light	when	snouts	owl
	lights	who	sounds	plow
	night	would		sows
	o'clock	you	**"ar" words:**	town
	of		barn	wow
	one		barnyard	yowled
	outside		far	
	perhaps		farm	
	put		farmer	
	she		star	
	so		stars	